The Penguin and the Dinosaur

words and pictures by

Kevin Herring

For my grandchildren

Oliver, Dexter, Eva and William

This is the story of a young king penguin called Dipper and his daring adventure.

On a cold winter morning, near the very bottom of our planet Earth, the penguin colony were having a BIG meeting.

The colony were talking about things.
Important things like keeping warm
and fishing and where would be a
good place to lay some eggs.

But mostly about keeping warm.

All of Dipper's family and friends were there.

The meeting was going on for a long time and, although it is good to talk about important things, Dipper was getting a bit bored and so he decided to go for a little walk.

None of the other penguins noticed that Dipper was
walking further and further away and
heading off into the distance.

After a while, Dipper noticed a strange mark in the snow.

It was a very big mark and he had never seen anything like it before.

He studied it carefully and decided it must be a footprint.

"But who would leave a footprint SO big?" he said to himself.

He walked on and found another footprint and then another.

There was a huge space between each one and Dipper was confused.

Now, Dipper was quite a clever little penguin, so he started to try and think who the footprints could belong to.

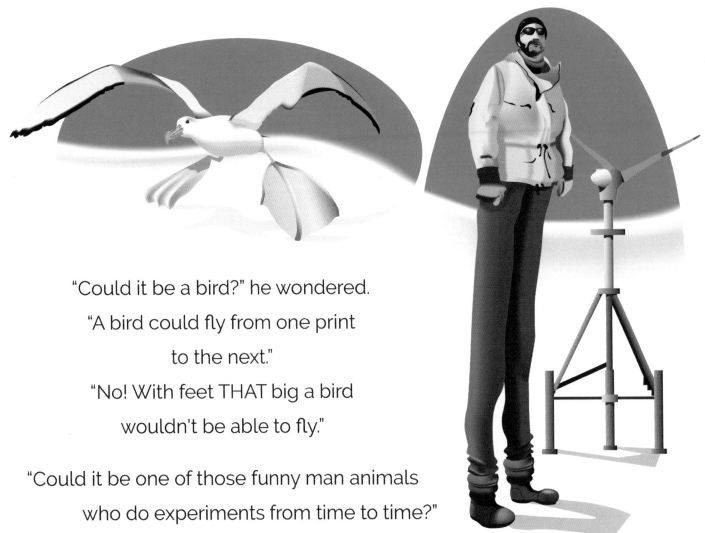

"Could it be a bird?" he wondered.
"A bird could fly from one print
to the next."
"No! With feet THAT big a bird
wouldn't be able to fly."

"Could it be one of those funny man animals
who do experiments from time to time?"
"No! A man would have to have very very long
legs to reach from one print to another."

No matter what strange animals Dipper thought of,
and some of them were very strange indeed,
there were none that could have made the prints.

He had to admit he didn't know, so he just kept walking
and following the footprints.
It wasn't too long before he realised he was completely lost.
"I can follow the footprints back to where I came from"
he thought to himself, sensibly.
But, when he looked back, they had almost been completely
covered by the snow blowing over them as he walked past.

Dipper felt cold and frightened and sad and lonely.

But mostly cold.

However, he was an adventurous penguin and decided

he would carry on and 'hope for the best.'

As he walked on, he looked around at all the strange and

wonderful shapes that had been made by the snow

and the ice and the rocks and the wind and the sea.

There were great arches and slopes and tall mountains.

Icicles that went up and icicles that went down.

There was even a big, smooth, oval shaped rock with green and red lines all over it that was squeezed underneath a ledge.

After quite some time, just as Dipper was
thinking how beautiful everything was,
he heard a tremendous ROOAAAR!

What he thought was one of the
arches he had seen had moved,
shaken the snow off of its back,
neck and head and was
staring down at Dipper in a
very serious way!

Dipper had never seen anything so big,

so strange or so dangerous.

"WHOO ARE YOUU?" it asked in a very deep voice.

Dipper was scared and wanted to run away, but he was also a
brave penguin and, looking up, said in a bold but ever-so-slightly
shaky voice "I'm Dipper the penguin. I'm very sad because I've
wandered away from my family and now I'm lost.
Would you be so kind as to tell me who you are please?"

The huge creature was surprised that this little penguin
had not run off and, in a quiet voice (which, even so,
was still quite loud), replied "My name is Solo.
I am a dinosaur and you are the first animal ever to see me.
I have been hiding here for many many years.
I am also very sad because I have mislaid my one and
only egg and can't find it anywhere."

"Maybe I can help you find it" Dipper said,
hoping the dinosaur wouldn't mind.
Solo liked this brave little penguin. "If I can't find it,
do you really think a small creature like Dipper can?"
she asked with a smile.

Dipper was disappointed and his head dropped.
Looking at Solo's feet, he noticed that the big footprints
he had seen earlier were, of course, hers.
"What does your egg look like?"
he asked, determined not to give up.

Solo was impressed with her new friend, "It is a big, smooth, oval shape with green and red lines all over it" she said.

"I've seen it, I've seen it!!" shouted Dipper, very excitedly. "I have been following your footprints and noticed your egg squeezed underneath a ledge. The trouble is, your footprints have now been covered up, so I don't know which direction to go" he said, feeling suddenly sad again.

"Oh, I know exactly which way I have been"
Solo replied with a very happy look.
"If you take me to the ledge and
find my egg, I will show you
the way back to your family!"

Dipper was delighted.
"Yes, yes" he replied excitedly,
"Let's go now!"

"OK" said Solo "But you must never tell any other penguin
that you have seen me, This will be our secret."

With everything agreed, Dipper and Solo set off in the direction they had been and it wasn't too long before Dipper found the ledge and, stuck underneath it as he had promised, was the egg!

Solo was so happy and relieved and very pleased with Dipper.

"Thank you SO much!" she said,

"Let me help you get up on my back and I'll take you home."

Once Dipper had struggled up onto Solo's back, the dinosaur shouted "Hold on tight, let's go!"

Dipper did indeed have to hold on very tight, as Solo was running as fast as a dinosaur could, taking massive strides through the snow.

It wasn't too long before they got near to Dipper's home.
Even the colony had heard Solo's roar from far away, which had
brought a sudden end to their meeting and it was then that
they had realised that Dipper was missing.

He wasn't up there...

and he wasn't
over there...

and he wasn't down
there either!

They had all been searching for him ever since.

Hidden behind a hill, Dipper carefully jumped down
from the huge dinosaur and promised not to tell
the other penguins about Solo.

Dipper and Solo said goodbye and thanked
each other for what they had done.

As Solo merrily walked back to her hiding place with her egg,
the happy little penguin ran off to his family and friends.

They were all thrilled to see him again!

Dipper was finally home, cold and hungry and tired.

But mostly cold.

After a lot of hugs from his
family to warm him up,
he enjoyed a big and tasty
fish supper and had
a very long sleep.

The End

25025115R00019

Printed in Poland
by Amazon Fulfillment
Poland Sp. z o.o., Wrocław